sleepover Girls

Sleepover Girls is published by Capstone Young Readers
A Capstone Imprint
1710 Roe Crest Drive
North Mankato, Minnesota 56003
www.capstoneyoungreaders.com

Library of Congress Cataloging-in-Publication Data is available
on the Library of Congress website.
ISBN: 978-1-4342-9757-0 (library binding)
ISBN: 978-1-62370-195-6 (paperback)
ISBN: 978-1-4342-9765-5 (eBook)

Summary: Being a twin has its perks (especially when your twin is a
boy). This year, Willow and Winston are holding their first ever co-ed
birthday party, and everyone in class is invited. This means Win's cute
friend Jacob is on the guest list. Willow's pumped that her crush will be
coming over and gets the Sleepover Girls to help her plan a party that's
all kinds of awesome! But even the best-laid plans can go awry. Jacob
seems to like Ashley, and mean girls Franny and Zoe are driving Willow
nuts. Can the birthday girl pull it together and throw a memorable party,
or will her birthday be a complete bust?

Designed by Tracy McCabe

Illustrated by Paula Franco

Printed in China by Nordica
0414/CA21400619
032014   008095NORDF14

Willow's BOY-CRAZY BIRTHDAY

by Jen Jones

capstone
young readers

Maren Melissa Taylor

Maren is what you'd call "personality-plus" —
sassy, bursting with energy, and always ready
with a sharp one-liner. She dreams of becoming
an actress or comedienne one day and moving
to Hollywood to make it big. Not one to fuss
over fashion, you'll often catch Maren wearing a
hoodie over a sports tee and jeans. She is an only
child, so she has adopted her friends as sisters.

Willow Marie Keys

Patient and kind, Willow is a wonderful
confidante and friend. (Just ask her twin,
Winston!) She is also a budding artist with
creativity for miles. She will definitely own
her own store one day, selling everything she
makes. Growing up in a hippie-esque family,
Willow acquired a Bohemian style that
perfectly suits her flower child within.

Delaney Ann Brand

Delaney's smart and motivated — and she's
always on the go! Whether she's volunteering
at the animal shelter or helping Maren with her
homework, you can always count on Delaney.
You'll usually spot low-maintenance Delaney in
a ponytail and jeans (and don't forget her special
charm bracelet, with unique charms to symbolize
each one of the Sleepover Girls). She is a great
role model for her younger sister, Gigi.

Ashley Francesca Maggio

Ashley is the baby of a lively Italian family.
Her older siblings (Josie, Roman, Gino, and Matt)
have taught her a lot, including how to get
attention in such a big family, which Ashley has
become a pro at. This fashionista-turned-blogger
is on top of every style trend and shares it with
the world via her blog, Magstar. Vivacious and
mischievous, Ashley is rarely sighted without
her beloved "purse puppy," Coco.

chapter One

Twindom definitely has its perks — and pitfalls. Trust me, I should know. I'm one-half of Willow and Winston Keys (the double Ws). And, at the current moment, my beloved other half was both annoying me *and* also secretly helping me out. How? Well, he kept stepping on the backs of my moccasins, which was beyond irritating. But I didn't mind because one of his besties, Jacob Willis, had ended up walking home from school with us. And let's just say I wouldn't mind if Jacob was Winston's bestie and my boyfriend.

Thwap! Winston stepped on the back of my shoe again, and I tripped forward as my shoe came off. "Win!" I cried, grabbing it off the ground and hitting him with it. "Knock it off. Seriously."

He snatched the shoe back and threw it over to Jacob. "Pickle in the middle!" he yelled, throwing it back and forth with Jacob. I just stood there with my arms folded, blushing like a dork. It was just like Win to completely embarrass me in front of Jacob. Cute, dark-haired Jacob, rocking a casual style and black-rimmed glasses.

Luckily, my friend Ashley decided to step in and save the day. She swung her giant pink handbag in the air, blocking the shoe, and in a classic Ash move, it fell right into the purse!

"Game over, boys," she said, giving it back to me. "Here you go, Wills. And Win, really? Pickle in the middle? I didn't know we were five years old again."

I gave her a grateful look. If I could be one-tenth as confident as Ashley, I'd probably have a much better chance with Jacob. "I guess it's really true what they say about girls being way more mature than guys," I joked.

Winston made a face. "Is that why you still have your American Girl doll?" he teased me. I felt myself blush again and made a mental note to turn my American Girl doll into a voodoo doll with his name on it. Most of the time, we got along okay, but he was really on a roll today.

Instead of having a good comeback for him like usual, I felt totally tongue-tied in front of Jacob. (That was nothing new.) Thank goodness Ashley was always right there with a sassy saying, and once again, she didn't let me down. "Oh, so *that's* what I saw you playing with during Willow's last sleepover," she joked.

Jacob's ears perked up before Winston could retort. "Sleepover?" he asked. "Why wasn't I invited?"

Ashley pushed him playfully. "Maybe you should go look for that invite that got 'lost' in the mail."

I giggled. *That* invite wasn't going to happen anytime soon. As big of a crush as I had on Jacob, the idea of him crashing one of our sleepovers wasn't really that appealing. The reason was simple: our Friday night sleepovers were sacred girl time!

For about as long as I could remember, Ashley and I had been spending Friday nights with Delaney and Maren (and, lately, sometimes our new friend Sophie). Though we rotated houses, one thing was always the same: the ridiculous amount of fun that we had.

As for Winston, I had to hand it to him —
as annoying as he could be, he was usually a
pretty good sport when the fab four invaded
our household.

And, on that note, we'd arrived at our street,
which meant (sadly) saying *sayonara* to Ash and
Jacob. "See ya tomorrow, bro," said Winston.

"Later, guys," said Jacob. "I'll walk you home
the rest of the way, Ashley." Aww, spoken like
a true gentleman. Yet another reason to crush
on him.

Once they were out of sight and we were
headed down our street, I faced Winston
defiantly. "Why do you insist on torturing me?"
I asked, pouting.

A grin spread across Winston's face. "You
totally *like* Jacob, don't you?" he said. I shook
my head "no" quickly, but he wasn't having it.
"Willow loves Jacob, Willow loves Jacob," he
sang, over and over again.

"Will you *please* drop it?" I asked. I knew there was no use lying to him. We knew each other way too well. It was part of that whole twin thing. "If you don't, I'll tell Mom how you almost got detention the other day. Oh, and I guess that would mean getting grounded from video games again."

"Don't you dare," he said. "Race you home!" He took off with a head start up the hill, but I still managed to come in first as we breathlessly hit our driveway. Those long legs of mine did come in handy *sometimes*.

Being fraternal twins, I was actually a little bit taller than Winston; in fact, I was taller than almost all of the guys in our class. It was pretty awkward most of the time. (And don't even get me started on trying to find pants that aren't too short!)

Anyway, the simple act of arriving at home chilled me out a little. Even if I *weren't* a homebody (which I am), it'd be hard not to love our house. Our parents were all about being "one with nature," so they'd designed the house to be an indoor-outdoor oasis. One of my fave things about it was the glass atrium right in the center with a giant tree growing through it. The back of our house has floor-to-ceiling windows, which gives us a killer view of the valley. You could usually find me vegging out in my dad's recliner, listening to music and staring out the window.

But today my mom was sitting in my usual spot. She had two smoothies waiting for us as well. "Hey, Mom! You're home early," I exclaimed. My parents ran a health store called Creative Juices, so they had to work a lot.

"What can I say? I missed my terrific twosome," she said, handing us her newest smoothie creations. "Here, I made you guys pumpkin swirls." One of the tastier perks of having parents that ran a juice business was being a tester for the new creations.

"Thanks, Mom," said Winston, flopping onto the couch. "Did you put the vitamin B-12 shot in there this time? You always claim it helps concentration, so maybe it'll help me do better on my boring science homework."

She ruffled his hair. "You know it," she said. "Now you have no excuses." My parents were pretty strict with us about our schoolwork.

I took a sip and was rewarded with pumpkin-y goodness. "Yummmm!" I said, slurping up even more. "This is amazing!"

"Yep, it's Octoberific," agreed Winston. He and I loved to come up with funny analogies for the way the juices and smoothies tasted.

"You are correct, brother," I said with a fake accent. "It's like autumn in a glass."

"Why yes, sister," he responded. "It most definitely is. A pumpkin patch of goodness."

My mom grinned. "Well, actually, that was what I wanted to talk to you two about," she said. "It's practically Halloween, and we still haven't talked about what we're going to do for your birthdays."

Birthdays were a big deal in our house — after all, there was double the reason to celebrate! Usually, Winston and his friends went out and did something like mini-golf or paintball, but I tended to stick with the tried-and-true: a sleepover with my besties. However, I usually get to have a two-night sleepover for my birthday, which is extra special. Plus, we always did another party with our extended family.

"Yeah, we'll have to pick a date for the two-night sleepover," I agreed. I was already mentally planning which chick flicks to watch. And maybe we could do pumpkin carving! I'd already been painting a bunch of pumpkins and putting them out on the front porch. Art was my favorite thing in the whole world, and I always had something creative happening.

My mom looked thoughtful. "Well, actually, your Dad and I thought this year you two could have a co-ed birthday party," she suggested. "It might be fun to invite a bunch of your classmates and do a big Halloween costume party. Plus, it would make things a lot easier on your dad and me to do both parties at once."

Winston lit up at the thought. "Are you kidding me?" he said. "That would be awesome!"

That was easy for him to say — he was totally outgoing. As for me, aka "the shy one," I wasn't sure how to feel. Being the center of attention always made me uneasy, and having a big party was very, well, un-me. On the other hand, I knew Ashley, Maren, and Delaney would be super-jazzed to help me plan, and there was always the Jacob factor, which was a huge bonus! And it was about time I tried to get out of my social comfort zone, or at least that's what I kept telling myself.

So that left just three words for my verdict: "Count me in."

chapter Two

I fidgeted excitedly in my seat as my mom started the car. It was time to go meet the other Sleepover Girls at our middle school's football game, and I couldn't wait to share the big news about my birthday soiree! None of us had ever had a co-ed birthday party before, so I knew they'd be crazy excited about it.

But once I joined the girls in the stands, it was hard to get a word in edgewise! Ashley couldn't stop talking about *her* crush, Grant Thompson, and how he was killing it out on the field. Delaney was obsessing over her latest campaign for student council, trying to get a recycling program approved for the cafeteria. And Maren was all abuzz about the trip she and her mom were busy planning to Vancouver. (Her mom had a super-cool job as a travel magazine editor.) As the quiet one of the group, I was used to it. It was far from the first time I'd been unable to break through the chatter.

"Go big D!" Ashley yelled, springing up from her seat to cheer on the defense. We were playing Springville Middle, and they were very close to scoring and taking the lead. Ashley adjusted her plaid scarf nervously, biting her lip as the team went for the fourth down. It was funny to see Ash so invested in the game.

Usually Maren was our sports nut, but Grant seemed to be making a diehard football fan out of Ashley.

"Yeah!" we all screamed when the ref signaled that our team had successfully held them back and would reclaim possession of the ball. I wasn't really that into football, but the spirit was kind of contagious. And sitting outside enjoying the crisp autumn weather was just a bonus.

"Sounds like Grant heard you cheering for him. Maybe he thought you said, 'Go big 'G,'" joked Maren, getting a giggle out of all of us. She was always our dose of comic relief.

Ashley grinned. "Whatever it takes," she said, waving a floppy red and gold pom in the air as we all sat down again.

It seemed like I finally had my "in" to tell everyone about the big co-ed birthday party. "So, Ash, you might have your chance to hang out with Grant outside of school," I told her eagerly. "My parents want me and Winston to have a double birthday party. We were thinking of doing a Halloween costume type of thing."

"What? This is amazing news! Talk about burying the lead!" Delaney exclaimed. Ever since she'd started writing for the school newspaper, she loved to use phrases like that. (Delaney was our "joiner" of the group. Since we'd gotten to middle school, she'd joined as many groups as she could fit into her schedule.)

Ashley's eyes widened, and her face spread into a giant grin. "Understatement, Laney!" she said. "Willow, your birthday is going to be epic! Now I'm *really* going to have to come up with an awesome costume."

Maren looked excited. "I already know what I'm going to be," she said smugly. "Can you say *Pink Power Ranger?*" She struck a cheesy fight pose.

We all looked at each other and yelled, "It's Morphin Time!" Watching re-runs of the old show was one of our favorite guilty pleasures on Saturday mornings after our sleepovers.

Our loud outburst caught the attention of Franny and Zoey Martin, who were sitting just a few rows ahead of us. Having been nicknamed the "Prickly Pair" for their, well, prickly demeanor, the twins were not on the list of our favorite peeps.

Franny turned around with a superior look. "You guys still watch that show?" she said, rolling her eyes. "How . . . cute." I made another mental note to kill Winston if he ever told the Prickly Pair about my American Girl doll.

"You know it!" answered Maren. "It's retro-tastic. Sorry we don't sit around on Saturday mornings and listen to classical music and drink tea." She waved her pinky finger in the air to make her point.

"Whatever, Power Ranger," said Zoey. But she was smiling. "What *are* you guys doing for Halloween, anyway? Did I hear you say you were having a party, Willow?"

We all kind of looked at each other uncomfortably. I hadn't exactly made the guest list yet, and I knew that, if the other girls had their way, the twins wouldn't make the cut. However, I was always a big softie — and a terrible liar. "Oh, um, yeah, I am," I said slowly. I could see Delaney out of the corner of my eye trying to shake her head "No!" without them seeing, but I couldn't help myself. "Winston and I are having a costume party to celebrate our birthdays."

Most of my sentence got drowned out as Ashley screamed, "Touchdown, Tigers!" and everyone jumped up and started cheering. (Except the Prickly Pair, who were always too cool for school.)

"Whew, saved by the score," I heard Delaney mutter under her breath. I'm sure she wasn't too thrilled that I'd told Franny and Zoey about the party, but I couldn't help it. I wasn't going to lie.

As everyone else was freaking out over our big score, I started freaking out about the party. Should I invite everyone in the class? Invite only close friends? Just let Win invite a bunch of people while I go into hiding? I knew one thing: I didn't want to make anyone feel bad. I was going to have to do some thinking on how to be the hostess with the mostest — even if that meant partying with the Prickly Pair.

chapter Three

On Friday, most people say, "TGIF!" But not me — I say "TGISD!" (Thank goodness it's sleepover day!) This week, it was Delaney's turn to have us all over to her house, and I, for one, couldn't wait. Win had been driving me *crazy* all week, and I've been totally stressed thinking about the party. My birthday was just a few weeks away, so I couldn't wait to have a planning meeting with the girls and get the wheels in motion!

Delaney greeted me at the door with a pumpkin-shaped basket full of candy. "I'm getting into the Halloween spirit early," she giggled. "Here, take some." She thrust it out toward me.

"Don't mind if I do!" I exclaimed, grabbing a few Kit-Kats. I tended to eat super-healthy since that's the way I grew up, but here and there I had some chocoholic tendencies. You can't blame a girl, especially in times of stress, right?

Suddenly I got grabbed from behind and let out a huge scream. "Got you!" yelled Maren. "Sorry, Wills," she said, patting my shoulder apologetically. "I couldn't resist."

I tried to catch my breath. "I see that," I replied, laughing. "Excuse me while I go check into the hospital for signs of a heart attack."

Maren just laughed. "A heart attack? Really? It's not like you to be so dramatic about things."

I giggled as we moved inside. "Is Ashley here yet?" I flung my striped duffel onto the oversized couch, causing Delaney's dog Frisco to jump up and sniff the contents.

Delaney scooped her little pup up in her arms. "She went shopping with Sophie after school," she answered. "There was some big sale at the outlet mall. I'm sure she'll be here soon. Although those two *do* have some pretty impressive shopping stamina."

Ashley was a true fashion addict, so that was no surprise. Sophie was a new friend of hers who had moved to town not too long ago, and they'd immediately bonded over their shared clothing obsession. It had taken the rest of us Sleepover Girls a bit longer to warm up to Sophie, but we'd eventually come around. And I was glad we did! She was pretty cool once she opened up, and it was nice to have another girl in our group.

Delaney's mom brought us out some pretzel crisps and kettle corn. We got all comfy, and Delaney turned on some tunes. Now *this* was what I call the perfect way to relax. I was so relaxed I almost forget about the party stress, which was just what I needed.

"Willow, can I do a fishtail braid on your hair while we wait for Ash?" Maren asked. The girls loved to do fun and weird styles on my long blond hair since it went all the way down my back. (Blame the whole hippie parents thing. Even Winston had long-ish hair.)

"You know it!" I told her. "Just no hair color, and we'll be all good." We all laughed, remembering our recent beauty disaster at Sophie's sleepover. Sophie and her sister had talked Ashley into trying some colorful streaks that ended up looking more like a little kid's Crayola project. We'd been a lot more careful with DIY beauty tips ever since.

"Well, since we're waiting around, do you want to start brainstorming some ideas for your party, Willow?" Delaney asked. "I can take notes." She whipped out a hot pink notepad. Delaney was always prepared, which was just one of the many reasons I loved that girl.

I nodded happily. "Sure!" I exclaimed. "I need all the help I can get." And I knew my girls were just the ones to give it to me. Sure enough, Delaney had tons of ideas on how to get started. She made a little spreadsheet in her notebook with categories like decorations, food, games, and other cool party stuff. We started making lists and brainstorming like crazy. It didn't seem as overwhelming with everyone helping.

"What if we play poker with candy?" said Maren. "I bet I could get a pretty good haul of goodies, as I am quite the poker player."

"More like the Joker!" Delaney replied with a laugh. "That would be fun, but there's way too many people to do something like that unless we do a tournament."

It didn't seem like the right fit. "Nah," I said. "It's a cool idea, but I think it would take up too much time. We should definitely play some games, though!"

Maren snorted. "If Ash has her way, we'll all be stuck playing 'Spin the Bottle,'" she said. I knew my parents would never be down for *that,* but I still felt myself blush at the thought of kissing Jacob, even if it was just for a silly game.

Then, as if on cue, we heard Ashley's signature knock at the door (four quick ones with a doorbell at the end) — now the sleepover could *really* get started! "Greetings, girlies," she said, popping her head through the door before Delaney could answer. "Did I hear my name?"

We all giggled. Busted. We caught Ash up on our ideas, and she had plenty of her own to add into the mix. From mummy-wrapped hot dogs to apple bobbing to a candy scavenger hunt, there was no shortage of fun stuff to do. Maren even had the fun idea of dangling a pair of legs with striped stockings inside the fireplace, like a witch was hanging in there. I was surprised by how excited I was. Maybe this whole hostess thing wouldn't be so bad after all.

"Oh, one more question before we move on to movie time. Can anyone come over and help make the invitations tomorrow afternoon?" I piped up. "It's too late to start tonight."

Delaney frowned. "Oh, man, I would, but I'm volunteering at the shelter tomorrow," she explained. She was super-dedicated to her work at the animal shelter. No surprise there, since that's where she'd found Frisco.

"I have to go to Roman's robotics match," said Ashley, doing a little "robot" dance move. "Their team made a robot that can kick a soccer ball or something crazy like that." Coming from a big family with four brothers and one sister, Ashley often spent her weekends doing stuff with her fam.

We all looked at Maren expectantly. "Need you even ask?" said Maren, breaking into a grin. "Of course I'll come help you. Is Winston going to help, too?"

"He'd better," I said. "It's his party too."

"Speaking of invites, Willow, did you decide to invite the Prickly Pair?" Delaney asked.

I hesitated, but figured I might as well get it out in the open now. "Yep, turns out we're going to invite everyone in our grade," I admitted. "You know what they say — go big or go home." That had seemed like the fairest approach that would cause the least amount of drama.

Delaney shrugged. "Oh boy, well, this should be interesting! I can't wait to see what costume they come up with this year," said Delaney. Unlike Winston and I, who never dressed identical, Franny and Zoey *always* did the mirror image thing.

"Maybe they'll dress as Siamese twins," giggled Maren. "They're already attached at the hip anyway."

I was glad that the girls had a sense of humor about it; in fact, they even seemed excited at the thought of me having such a big party. And as we settled in to watch a scary movie in preparation for Halloween, I got even more excited about the party. Things were really looking up!

chapter Four

"Whoa, that thing is serious," exclaimed Maren as I pulled out my crafting kit the next morning. I'd recently transformed one of my dad's old fishing tackle boxes into my "box of tricks," and it had everything from glittery Mod Podge to scallop scissors to lace inside. What can I say? I was a crazy crafter at heart.

"And I have two more boxes of supplies in the basement if we need them," I told her.

She shook her head. *"That's* doubtful," she said, eyeing my collection and dancing a little bit in her chair. "Okay, let's do this!"

I nodded excitedly and set out each of the components of the invite into neat piles. I'd found a really cute accordion-folded spiderweb invite idea online, and I was super-pumped to make some invite magic.

Now, if only Winston would come down and help us. He hadn't done a thing to help with the party yet, and this was something he could handle.

"Hold on," I told Maren. "Let me go get Win. He's not getting out of this!" I bounded up the steps two at a time.

"Hey. Maren is here and ready to help with the invitations. Can you come down and help?" I asked nicely.

"Nope," he answered, barely looking up from his book. "Jacob's on his way over and we're going to play video games."

Typical Winston! He'd totally forgotten that we were supposed to get party stuff ready today. As usual, I'd have to do all the hard work and he would get to have all the fun. Not this time — I was going to stand my ground. But wait a minute . . . did he just say *Jacob* was coming over? That sure made my day a little brighter.

"Well, that's funny, because I thought you were going to help me put together the invitations," I grumbled. "Oh well, I guess now you and Jacob can help."

He laughed. "Sure, after we play about five rounds of Madden we'll come down," he said, rolling his eyes. So much for supportive brothers! And I couldn't complain to my parents, because my mom and dad were at the shop.

I went back downstairs, totally annoyed. "Looks like we are on our own," I grumbled.

"What's up with Win?" Maren asked.

I explained that he was being super lame and would rather veg out with video games than help us. Maren looked a little disappointed, which was weird. Usually she and Winston drove each other crazy even more than he and I did! So I was probably just imagining that she was bummed.

I didn't get a chance to ask though, because Jacob barged into the house about two seconds later. As always, he looked super cute. He had on a basic white T-shirt with slouchy jeans, and his signature rimmed glasses made him look delightfully dorky and hip.

"Good afternoon, ladies," he said as he did a dramatic bow. He's smart and funny. Dreamy.

I grinned. "Hi Jacob," I said. I know he's just a normal boy, but I get so shy around him.

Maren gestured to our table full of stuff. "Any chance you want to help us make these invitations?" she said. "You know you want to."

Jacob grinned. "Yes, that's how I'm dying to spend my Saturday," he teased. "I don't even know what costume to wear to this party. I bet Ashley would have some good ideas since she's so into clothes and stuff. Where is she, anyway?"

I explained that she was spending the day at her brother's robotics match, trying to ignore the voice that told me Jacob always seemed to be focused on Ashley's whereabouts.

"Ahh, got it," Jacob replied. "Later, gators!" And with that, he bounded up the steps to see Winston.

I felt myself swoon as my overactive brain started daydreaming about us dressing up as a couples' costume. Romeo and Juliet? Frankenstein and the bride of Frankenstein? Ken and Barbie? Bonnie and Clyde? Kermit and

Miss Piggy? We could even do something funny like ketchup and mustard or eggs and bacon. The possibilities were endless. But the actual chances? Less than slim to none.

"Willow, snap out of it!" said Maren. "We've got work to do." I grinned sheepishly. Caught in the act. I couldn't help it — Jacob made me all gushy.

Once I was able to focus, we were able to get a pretty good system going. I trimmed all the orange and black cardstock to be the right shape and folded it together so it was perfectly lined up. Maren punched out the spider shapes and glued them to the front of the invites. I was definitely in my element! It was relaxing to be so "in the zone."

That is, until something totally terrifying happened. "Think fast!" yelled Winston, appearing out of nowhere to empty a cup of live spiders on top of our workspace. "We thought you needed some help with your invitations." The giant hairy spiders started scurrying all over the table!

"*Aaaaahhhhhhhhh!*" I screamed, jumping up and knocking over my chair. "Get them away! I can't believe you!"

Since we lived near the woods, there were always humongous spiders in our garage and backyard. I'm fine with spiders outside, but it is not okay to bring them into our home! Winston obviously thought it was funny to invite them *inside*.

Jacob and Winston were doubled over laughing at me and Maren, who were clutching onto each other for dear life. She was screaming even louder than me! Winston picked up by one of the spiders by the leg and started chasing us around the room with it.

"What on earth is going on here?" bellowed my dad from the doorway. He and my mom stood there, looking none too happy with all the screaming and mess. Winston stopped dead in his tracks, speechless for once.

"Ask Spiderman," I said, glaring at Winston. Jacob picked up on the tension and grabbed his backpack.

"I think that's my cue to take off," he said. "See you guys Monday at school."

Maren wasn't far behind. "Call me if you need anything, Wills," she said, following Jacob out the door. "I'm only a bike ride away!"

After my dad made Winston collect all of the spiders and take them outside (where they belonged!), we had a family meeting in the den.

"This is probably a good time to go over some ground rules for the party," said my mom sternly. "We'll start with cleanup duty. Winston, since you didn't bother helping your sister today and decided to play a prank on her instead, you'll be doing whichever cleanup chores Willow doesn't want to do — without complaining."

Ha! Score one for me. The rest of their rules were pretty basic, such as keeping certain rooms off-limits, pitching in for party prep, and all the usual stuff. All stuff I had no prob with, and hopefully Winston would behave himself, too. Maybe he would even help out a little more now that mom and dad talked to us, but I highly doubted it.

chapter Five

Witches and zombies and mermaids, oh my! The Halloween superstore was seriously a wonderland of crazy costumes; just being inside of it got me even more pumped for Halloween. I could see by the looks on the other girls' faces that they felt exactly the same way. Just one week away from the par-tay, and we were on a mission to find the perfect costumes.

"What do you girls think of this one?" asked Maren, holding up a ghost costume. "Isn't it just boo-tiful?"

Sophie giggled. We'd invited her along on our shopping excursion, because, let's be honest, it's not shopping unless Sophie's involved! "Ghosts are so last year," she joked. "I think we can find a better costume for you. Something that really screams Maren."

Delaney pulled something off the rack and giggled. "I've got it!" she said, holding up a Little Orphan Annie costume. "Does this bring back memories?"

Oh, boy, did it. Back in our elementary school days, we'd done a school production of "Annie," where Maren had (naturally) been the redheaded rock star in the lead role. Delaney had played her dog, Sandy. While most girls would never want to play the part of a dog, this was a fitting role for our favorite animal lover!

Delaney still claims it's the best work she's ever done in a play. True to form, I'd been backstage painting props, where I was most at home.

Now it was Maren's turn to giggle. "Now *that* is so yesterday," she said. "I'll stick with my Pink Power Ranger costume. I think my orphan days are long gone."

Plays had been kind of a sore subject lately in our little group, as Sophie had snagged the role of the Mad Hatter in this year's production of *Alice in Wonderland*. Maren was super-bummed that she didn't get it at the time, but luckily, we'd all moved on.

Sophie picked up a white go-go boots and tried them on. "Love these!" she exclaimed. "What if I dressed up as a go-go dancer from the '60s? The style is to die for, and I could pull out some fun dance moves."

"I think you've found your costume, chica," said Ashley.

Sophie began posing with her boots and practicing some dance moves, but I got distracted as I spotted a familiar face across the store. "Isn't that Grant and his dad over there?" I asked, causing Ashley to duck suddenly behind a rack of costumes.

"Oh no! It totally is!" she said, frantic. "I didn't even do my hair today, and just look at this outfit!" Keep in mind that Ashley looks amazing no matter what she's wearing or how her hair is styled, so I wasn't sure why she was panicking.

Sophie ducked down to join her. "Here, I have the perfect solution," she said, slapping Ashley lightly across the face on both sides. "Now you've got great color and have forgotten about your hair and outfit. You can thank me later for my genius."

We didn't know whether to laugh or be disturbed at Sophie's "method," but Ash didn't look too startled. In fact, she started cracking up and pretty soon we were all laughing nonstop. We were laughing so hard that we didn't even notice that Grant was making his way over to us.

"Hey there," said Grant. "Fancy seeing you guys here. What's so funny?" He looked at us expectantly.

Ashley still looked embarrassed, so Maren jumped in quickly. "Grant, you're just in time!" exclaimed Maren. "We found the perfect costume for you." She handed him a princess costume, making all of us dissolve into laughter again.

A good sport, Grant took it from her and admired it. "You know me too well," he joked. "It really is my color. However, it might be a little small."

"So true," Maren said. "What are you going to be for the big party?"

"I guess you guys will just have to wait until Willow and Winston's party to see," he said with a smile. I thought Ashley was going to burst with happiness as she stared at him.

"Or we could just spy on you at the checkout counter," piped in Ashley, who seemed to have regained her sanity.

Grant grinned her way. "Yeah, but that wouldn't be any fun, would it?" he said. "See you guys." He went back to join his dad, leaving Ashley swooning.

"Okay, he is *beyond*," said Ash, all swept up in the moment. "I can't wait for him to see me in my costume, which I still need to find. Let's get moving, people!"

Seeing Ash so excited brought Jacob back into my head. Thanks to her, I'd gotten up the courage to hand our party invite personally to Jacob earlier this week. I was so grateful to her for helping me pass out the invites and even coming with me to give Jacob his. Of course, it was a no-brainer that he was going to come since he and Win were besties, but it was still weird seeing him without Win around.

Having Jacob on the brain had become pretty much a 24/7 thing at this point for me. But I couldn't really tell if he liked me back. I never got up the courage to talk to him long enough to find out!

"Earth to Willow," said Delaney, waving a costume in front of my face. "What do you think of this?" She'd picked out this super-cool, shiny blue Statue of Liberty costume — torch included! I instantly fell in love with it, even though the spiky crown would probably make me look even taller.

"Just call me Lady Liberty," I said, taking it from her. Maybe I could convince Win to be Uncle Sam! Though I was pretty sure he had his heart set on being C3PO from *Star Wars*.

Just like Jacob, Win was a bit of a movie geek. And he wasn't the only one, as Delaney soon settled on a lily-white Princess Leia costume. It was too perfect, as her brown braids would look awesome in twin coils! Delaney and Win would make quite the pair.

It took Ashley what felt like a year to settle on a costume, but she finally met her match. It was the coolest outfit ever. It was called Twister Girl! and was inspired by the classic game. The polka-dotted dress and spinner board hat looked absolutely adorable on her. Our resident fashionista was ready to hit the Halloween circuit in style. Her costume had a '60s glam vibe with killer boots, which was similar to Sophie's costume.

"Perfect! We'll almost be twinsies!" Ashley said to Sophie.

"Right on, girl. Looks like we're all good to go!" exclaimed Sophie. "Oh, but Willow, I forgot: there's one thing I need to ask you." She looked a little nervous.

"Shoot," I told her. I couldn't imagine what she'd have to ask that would freak me out, so I wasn't worried.

Sophie shifted from one foot to another. "Well, I happened to mention your sleepover campout before the birthday party to Franny and Zoey, and they kind of want to . . . come," Sophie said slowly. Clearly she was on much friendlier terms with them than we were.

I didn't know what to say. I didn't mind Franny and Zoey all that much, but the other girls thought they were the ultimate snobs. I didn't want my pre-party sleepover to be a disaster! But maybe it was a case of the more, the merrier? I decided to open up the decision to the group.

"Hmm, as long as my parents are cool with it, I guess it's okay," I said.

"Wait a minute," Delaney said, turning to Sophie with her arms crossed. "You're telling me Franny and Zoey want to come to Willow's house and camp out in *tents*? I have a hard time believing that!"

They did have a point. We had decided to do a campout instead of our regular inside sleepover in honor of the Halloween holiday, but the sleeping "in the wild" didn't really seem like the Prickly Pair's cup of tea.

"It's just like them to invite themselves to our party," Maren said. "I would never do that!"

Ashley had a bit more of an open mind about it. Maybe she was just in a great mood post-Grant encounter?

"Come on, guys. It'll make things interesting," she said. "Plus, they *did* hook Maren up with that autographed Luke Lewis CD not too long ago. It seems like they are trying to be nicer, and I think we should give them props for that."

Maren seemed to relent a bit. "True," she said. "It was pretty awesome of them to do that for me. All right, make room in the tent — the Prickly Pair is officially invited to join us."

This party (and preparty) was getting more interesting by the minute!

chapter Six

If there was one thing I'd learned over the last few weeks, it's that a hostess' work is truly never done. Between trying to keep up with school, checking to-do tasks off the seemingly endless party prep list, and silently stalking Jacob (at least I'm admitting it), the "fun" part of the party had yet to begin. It sure would help if my lovely twin brother would help, but I guess that was never going to happen.

Take dealing with the Prickly Pair for instance, which was proving to be a 24/7 job in itself. They'd stopped me after school the day I was supposed to go grocery shopping with my mom to pick up ingredients for the party treats.

"Hey, Maren," said Franny, cutting me off in the hallway. "We're sooo jazzed about your party and sleepover this weekend," finished Zoey. They often spoke in tandem. But I got it. Yet another twin thing.

"Me, too!" I told them. "It's going to be a blast, for sure." I started to move past them, since my mom was waiting outside in the car and I knew she was in a hurry. Time was always a–tickin' when you were counting down to party time!

"Wait, we wanted to run a few things past you," said Zoey, grabbing my arm. "I know it's Halloween and all, but can you make sure some of the recipes are healthy? We try really hard to eat healthy, and candy is *not* okay."

I grinned. "Um, do you know who you're talking to? I'm a health food junkie, too. Not to worry," I said, starting to head toward the doorway.

Franny stopped me in my tracks. "Well, can you make sure to get gluten-free foods? We don't 'do' wheat. Oh, and we're *obsessed* with seaweed snacks, so those would be great, too."

"Yeah, and we always drink green juice in the morning, so if you could pick up some of that, that would be fab," added Zoey.

I tried to hide my annoyance and take it in stride. High-maintenance was just how they rolled. "I'll have my mom make you the Verde Delight, straight from Creative Juices," I promised. "You've never tasted anything so green. Gotta run!"

Making the favors and accessories had been yet another adventure. Since there were more than 30 peeps who'd RSVP-ed that they were coming, it had been taking me forever to get all of the favors ready. Of course, who was I kidding? Being the obsessive crafter that I was, I probably was going a bit overboard.

The first things I made were orange "pumpkins," which were basically an orange tulle satchel filled with candy corn and tied with a curly green pipe cleaner at the top. The next favors were beaded necklaces to which I'd attached cool glow-in-the-dark skeletons at the end. I admit: after I put the necklaces together, I had gone totally overboard and painted the faces on the skeleton myself! I was hoping people would wear them during the party.

And the biggest project I'd tackled? The DIY party hats, jack-o-lantern grins, and funny sayings that I'd slaved over for the photo booth. The party hats looked like pieces of candy corn, while the jack-o-lantern grins were glued onto long sticks so people could hold them up and pose with them. (Forget mustaches — they were so last year!) I also had a few other props like glasses, hats, capes, and wands to go with the photo booth as well. We all know that the right props can make the best picture.

The flipside of all these bright ideas had been the time it had taken to make them. Hours after school every day was spent poring over my crafting kit, and I was still far from the finish line when Thursday rolled around. I know I should have asked for more help (especially from Winston since it was his party too), but I have a hard time letting go if things aren't perfect, so it was my own fault.

I was headfirst in a bin of crafting supplies when Winston came bounding into my bedroom. (Thankfully we had separate rooms, as he is as messy as he is lazy!)

"Sup, sis?" he said, flopping onto my zebra-striped comfy chair.

"Oh, not much, just my usual crafting craziness and getting everything ready for OUR party," I replied with some annoyance, flopping down next to him to take a break.

"I'm picking up some 'tude, dude," he replied. "If you want some help, you just need to ask. I'm sure I won't do things your way so you'll get mad anyway."

"I know, I know," I said with a sigh. "I'm just crabby. Where have you been all afternoon, anyway? You totally disappeared."

Winston squirmed a little. "Oh, I went to the comic book store with Maren," he said. "They had a launch party for the new *Wackadoodle #11* comic. The illustrator was there signing them. It was pretty sweet!"

It was hard to hide my surprise. For two people who usually traded insults like they were baseball cards, Winston and Maren sure seemed to be friendly lately.

"Well, isn't that interrrresting," I said. "Aren't you two the cutest little comic book couple?"

Winston's face turned a bright shade of crimson. "Whatever," he retorted. But he didn't deny it, which made me smile. "At least I'm not in love with Jaccccob."

Now it was my turn to blush. "Very funny," I said, returning to my crafting station so he wouldn't notice how embarrassed I was.

"Well, the feeling might be mutual," Winston offered. "He mentioned how pumped he was that you and Ashley personally invited him to the party."

I never really let myself entertain the thought that Jacob might actually like me back. However, we'd certainly spent tons of time together (thanks to Win), so I guess it wasn't totally out of the question.

"That was sweet of him," I said. "Maybe you could do a little detective work for me on that front, you know, just in case I *do* actually have a crush on him. Which I don't, of course."

Win shrugged. "What's in it for me?"

"Are you serious? I'm already doing all the work for this party, so don't push it," I said giving him a poisonous look. "Plus, Maren is one of my best friends obviously, so don't be so dumb."

He put his arms up and quickly gave in. "Okay, okay, I'll see what I can find out," he promised.

"Awesome!" I told him, handing him a pack of chalk. "Now go do up the driveway and make yourself useful for once."

"Yes, ma'am!" he said with a salute.

I'd had the bright idea to transform our driveway into a giant spiderweb, and I'd appointed Win in charge of making the vision come to life. And as I watched him out the window, I couldn't help but think how symbolic it was. Between Win and my bestie suddenly being lovey-dovey, my potential love connection with Win's BFF, and the Prickly Pair suddenly being part of our sleepover circle, life was starting to be one tangled web!

chapter Seven

For all of the worrying I'd done about throwing a big party, I'd barely had any time to feel shy about it. By the time Friday afternoon finally arrived, we had no choice but to go full steam ahead. The Sleepover Girls had come over to help me get all of the last-minute stuff done and set up shop in the kitchen to make some tasty treats.

With just a few hours before Sophie and the Prickly Pair arrived for the campout, we were determined to make the most of them!

But there was one of us who *wasn't* so keen on the whole cooking thing. "Can I just give moral support?" pleaded Maren. "I take after my mom. I'm about as useful in the kitchen as a bent spoon."

We all giggled. "Sure, chica," I told her. "So what if you're domestically disabled? Your presence alone is delish." And it was — without Maren's witty remarks, we'd probably all go batty (Halloween pun intended) trying to get it all done.

The deal I'd made with my parents was that the four of us would make finger foods and desserts, and they'd do the "heavy lifting" in the kitchen (including a signature party drink and some other yummy treats). Sounded pretty reasonable to me, until we actually got started.

I usually left the cooking to my parents, so I was a little clueless about what to do. Luckily, Ashley is from a huge Italian family who love to cook and eat. She is a pro when it comes to whipping up kitchen masterpieces.

She'd come prepared, too. "Just call me Martha Stewart," she said, pulling on a frilly yellow apron that read "Top Chef-in-Training" in bright red letters. Leave it to Ash to look adorable, even when it was just us girls.

Our first order of business? Pumpkin cupcakes and fried mac-and-cheese balls. (Hey, the health factor goes out the window a little when you're throwing a Halloween shindig.) We quickly got a good system going. Delaney and Ash were the cupcake queens, while I started to assemble the cheese balls. Once I had all the ingredients together in the pot, I even got Maren to help me stir it while I focused on other stuff.

Just as we were making some good progress, Winston burst into the kitchen, peeked his head over Maren's shoulder, and tried to dip his finger into the cheese mixture.

"Gross!" Maren yelled with a big smile on her face. "Get out of here."

But even as she said it, I could tell she didn't really mean it. It was just too weird to see the two of them flirt all the time!

"I'm going. I'm going. In fact, I'm on my way out to play catch," he said. "Wanna play?"

Maren looked at all of us, not sure what to say. I could tell she wanted to go, but didn't want to ditch out on kitchen duty. Even though I was a bit weirded out by her and my brother suddenly being so friendly, I didn't want to hold her back.

"Go!" I encouraged her, if only to stop the awkwardness of her and Win flirting. "Just turn off the burner, and I'll take over in a minute."

I could see her wheels turning. "Well, as long as you promise not to throw any spiders at me this time," she chided him.

I shuddered at the memory. "Yeah, Win, you still owe us for that one. Maybe you guys can even get the tents set up when you're done playing, you know, as a peace offering."

Winston reluctantly agreed, but Maren perked up a little at the thought of being helpful while ditching her kitchen duties. "Done dealio!" she said, leaving her guilt behind and replacing it with pure confidence. "All right, Win, prepare to see how a girl *really* throws."

As soon as they were gone, Ashley put down her rolling pin and gave us all an incredulous look. "Is it my imagination, or . . ." Ashley didn't have to finish her sentence. We all shared her flirt radar.

"I know," I finished for her. "I can't even go there! It's just too bizarre." Maren had always been totally grossed out by boys, and it seemed that was now changing — thanks to my oh so beloved brother.

We all crept toward the window, trying to be discreet (and quiet) as we spied on them in the backyard. Watching them play and laugh, I had to admit they'd be kind of cute together. Maren, tiny and petite with her red corkscrew curls, and tall, lanky Winston with his longish blond hair. Maybe she'd even be my sister-in-law one day! (Okay, I was probably getting a little ahead of myself. But still, it'd be a best-case scenario, and a girl can dream, right?)

Delaney wrinkled her nose like she detected a foul smell. Seconds later, we all smelled it, too. "What *is* that?" she said, stomping over to the food prep area. Peering onto the stovetop, she had her answer. "OMG," she said, holding up a burnt spatula. "Maren didn't turn off the burner when she went outside!"

I looked inside the pot and saw a melted plastic mess on top of our cheesy mixture. We were back at square one with the cheese balls and then some! I didn't know whether to laugh or cry. But, with us Sleepover Girls, the answer is always laugh, and pretty soon we were all holding our stomachs with laughter.

"She is so *dead!*" I managed to spit out between giggles.

"Don't kill her yet! Her ghost might haunt the party tomorrow!" joked Delaney. "It *is* Halloween, after all."

I frowned. "And we're down one dish," I said, totally discouraged. We didn't have enough ingredients to make another batch of the mac-and-cheese balls.

Always the resourceful one of the group, Delaney's fingers started flying over her iPad and soon she had a new recipe in mind. It was a giant cheese ball made out of mainly cream cheese and cheddar, perfect for dipping crackers. (You could also make it into a shape, so we made a ghost.)

I was still a little bummed that the mac-and-cheese balls had gone bust, but this sounded like a great alternative since my mom had all the right stuff in the fridge. I guess I would just have to make the mac-and-cheese balls for our next sleepover. This thought made me feel a lot better about everything and gave me some renewed energy to finish everything with a good attitude.

Just twenty minutes later, we were putting on the finishing touches, and the day had been saved. "Finito!" said Ashley, adding olive pieces onto our creation as the ghost's "eyes." It looked awesome, as if we'd planned it all along!

Grateful, I gave them both a hug for saving the day. "Looks boo-tiful," I assured them as we stored it in the refrigerator.

"And Maren doesn't get any," joked Delaney. At our shocked looks, she backed down. "I'm just kidding. Lighten up ladies."

I surveyed the kitchen with an approving glance. "Thanks to Team Top Chef-In-Training, there's plenty for everyone," I said.

We all high-fived to celebrate a job (kind of) well done — and getting one step closer to the fun part. Let the campout begin!

chapter Eight

"Here, this is perfect," whispered Ashley, pointing to a huge tree as we tiptoed through the woods behind my house later that night. The sun was almost all the way down, and Winston had somehow conned us into playing a game of flashlight tag. Of course, he was "it" since he loved terrorizing everyone and was the only boy around.

Originally Win was supposed to have some friends over as well, but that privilege got taken away when he pulled the spider prank. We could hear him counting to sixty loudly as we crouched down behind the old oak tree.

"Ready or not, here I come!" he bellowed, starting his mad dash through the backyard to catch all of us. Ashley and I tried to stifle our giggles at how dramatic and hyper he was.

A few moments later, I heard Franny and Zoey exclaim, "No fair!" It was obvious he'd caught them and they were out. No surprise there! They didn't want to get all dirty in the woods, so they'd probably hidden behind the tent or something totally obvious like that.

Just a few minutes later, we heard another "Gotcha!" as he busted Maren, Sophie, and Delaney, followed by them giggling like maniacs. It was official — Ash and I were the only ones left in the game.

I could see the flashlight scanning the backyard. The light was pretty far away so I was sure he hadn't even come close to figuring out our hiding spot. The flashlight started moving further away and Ashley and I cupped our hands over our mouths, trying to hide our giggles.

Crunch. Crunch. Crunch. I could hear the crispy sound of something walking on leaves in the woods behind us. I gulped, trying to reassure myself. There were no bears or coyotes or anything crazy around here like that . . . right?

The footsteps sounded like they were getting closer. I nudged Ashley to see if she heard it, too. She nodded, her eyes wide. Then, all of a sudden, something jumped out and grabbed us! *"Bwaaah!"* it yelled, causing me to jump out of my skin.

Totally freaked out, I tried to catch my breath. Crazy Winston! He'd snuck up on us without the flashlight. "You jerk!" I yelled at him, trying to catch my breath. "Are you trying to scare us to death?"

Win's face spread into a naughty grin. "No to death," he said. "I would miss you too much. Besides, you can blame Maren. She was the brilliant one who took the flashlight so I could fool you guys."

Ashley and I exchanged a look. This whole Winston-Maren BFF thing was really getting out of hand. "First the spatula disaster, and now the flashlight fiasco. Ms. Maren's on a roll this evening!" exclaimed Ashley.

Still somewhat startled, we stomped back to the tent area, where the girls had gathered and my dad was getting the fire started. "Another round of flashlight tag, anyone?" asked Winston with a huge smile on his face. "I'm down for some more, as I always enjoy scaring the crap out of you girls."

"I think I'd rather just have s'mores," said Delaney, eyeing the s'more fixings my mom had brought outside.

"Yeah, our flashlight tag game is totally *over*," I told Winston firmly. "You can go inside now. Hint. Hint."

He shrugged. "It's not really a hint if you have to say it. But I will do whatever you say, sister dearest," he said with a goofy British accent, bounding up the long steps to the deck. Oh, brother. We turned our attention to Maren, who was trying to stifle her laughter. These two are way more alike than I ever realized.

"Don't hate me," she said. "You have to admit it was funny."

Ashley folded her arms and rolled her eyes, but she was grinning. "I only hate you a little bit," she said, sticking out her tongue at Maren. The Prickly Pair just stood there looking at all of us like we were crazy.

All was forgiven once the fire was roaring and we were all happily roasting marshmallows. I'd pretty much given up on any semblance of healthy eating (it *was* my birthday, after all! I deserved a break), so I was definitely partaking. Plus, we'd even found gluten-free chocolate and graham crackers for the Prickly Pair, so I was pretty darn proud of myself. I definitely had to enjoy every moment.

"I think it's time for a game of Share or Dare," Sophie announced, putting down her stick to grab the basket full of "share" questions we had made earlier. We also had a basket of "dare" questions. Sophie had become pretty familiar with our sleepover traditions by now. It may seem weird to play Share or Dare instead of Truth or Dare, but we like to make things our own and really like the rhyme. Isn't it catchy? Plus it's super fun to pick a random question or dare out of the basket.

"We're game," said Franny and Zoey simultaneously. "Much better than being chased around by a crazy person with a flashlight," added Zoey.

"I'll even go first," said Franny, who was swaddled in a comfy Navajo blanket. I was surprised at how comfortable both her and Zoey seemed with our group. It was a nice surprise for all of us.

"Get ready for some fun!" said Sophie as she handed the "share" basket to Franny. She made a big show of digging around and pulled out a blue strip of paper.

But after she read the question, she exclaimed, "No way! I don't want to answer that!"

"Well, then you have to pick a dare from the basket," piped up Maren with a huge smile on her face. "Those are the rules."

Franny looked nervous, but nodded. Sophie looked excited as she handed the "dare" basket to Franny. Franny looked really nervous as she picked her dare. It was kind of funny to see Franny less than confident.

"Okay, here it is. You get to wrap me up in toilet paper like a mummy. Then I have to stand like that for three more turns," she said, getting a laugh out of all of us. "I can handle this!"

Surprisingly, Franny was up for it and was even laughing, and soon enough, she was fully mummified. Just her eyes peeked out from the roll of toilet paper we'd had a blast swaddling her up in.

"I want my mummy!" she joked, her words garbled from the toilet paper. It was strange — despite all of the demands, Franny and Zoey were actually turning out to be kind of okay. Well, so far, anyway. Even Maren seemed to finally accept them.

"Your turn to pick the next victim, Franny," said Maren.

"Okay, I pick . . . Delaney," said Franny. Maren handed the basket over to Delaney, who picked the "share" option.

"If you were stuck on a deserted island and could only bring one thing, what it would be?" read Delaney out loud. She didn't even need to think about that one. "That's a no-brainer. I would take Frisco! I never go anywhere without him, and plus, he could forage in the woods to find food for us."

That was our practical Delaney. It wasn't hard to picture her and Frisco living in harmony off in the middle of nowhere. Next it was Ashley's turn, and she didn't hesitate at all (but let's be honest — she rarely does unless it's something that involves Grant!)

"I'm in the mood for a dare!" she told Delaney. "Hit me with the basket."

Ashley picked a dare. She was quiet for a minute and then broke into a big smile.

"Call a boy you like just to say hi," she read. Ashley looked embarrassed and excited at the same time.

"Looks like Grant is going to be getting a phone call," said Sophie with a grin, handing Ashley her cell phone over. "Go for it!"

I could see Ashley's wheels turning as she dialed the number. But she must not have come up with anything too inspired, because as soon as Grant picked up, Ashley let out a long, loud fake burp into the phone and hung up! It was hilarious to see Ashley letting it all loose.

"I can't believe I just did that!" Ashley said as she collapsed into a pile of giggles along with everyone else. "Thanks to caller id he's totally going to know it was me!"

After we all recovered from our laugh attack, Maren was up. She fished a strip of paper out of the share basket, then turned even redder than her crimson curls.

"Read it to us!" urged Zoey, eager to hear what it said.

Maren cleared her throat, then stuttered out, "Do you currently have a crush on anyone? If so, whom?" I was really glad I hadn't gotten that question.

It was kind of funny to watch Maren squirm, especially since we all knew the answer. At all of our insistent stares, she finally broke down. "Okay! Okay! I might have a teeny-tiny crush on Winston," she admitted, looking down.

"*Awwww,*" we all exclaimed at once.

Maren crossed her arms, still mortified. "If you tell anyone else . . ." she began. We all assured her we'd take the secret to the grave — and Franny (who had finally busted free of her mummy wrap) and Zoey even seemed *sincere* about it. Go figure.

Eager to change the subject, Maren picked Zoey to go next. She pulled a strip, then looked thoughtful as she read the question out loud. "If a genie appeared and said you could have one wish, what would it be?"

Zoey looked down, a bit thrown off. We all leaned in a little closer to hear what she had to say. "I guess I wish that we could have a clean slate at school," she said in a rare vulnerable moment. "Everyone thinks we're these huge snobs, and it kind of bums me out. We really aren't like that."

None of us really knew how to respond. Let's face it, it was *true,* and the rep wasn't exactly undeserved. However, everyone deserves a second chance, and maybe tonight was the start of that. "Aww, Zoey," I said. "If it makes you feel any better, I'm really glad you're here tonight."

Maren chimed in, too. "Yeah, you definitely aren't as bad as I once thought." This made everyone laugh.

Franny put her arm around Zoey. "Plus, we can't help it if we're fabulous," she said, hugging her close. We all giggled, knowing that Franny wasn't totally kidding.

I took a deep breath. Between Maren's mega-crush and the Prickly Pair showing that they were human after all, things sure were shifting in our world.

chapter Nine

The game kept going: Zoey picked Delaney, Delaney picked Sophie, and Sophie picked me. I decided to do a dare — it was time to pep up this game a bit. "Okay, well, Winston's been driving you up the wall lately, right?" asked Sophie. At my nod, she went on, "Well, I dare you to get revenge on him right here, right now."

I racked my brain, trying to think of a good idea that wasn't *too* mean. Then, a light bulb moment. "I've got it!" I told the girls. "Follow me into my lair."

Once we were safely in my bedroom, I giggled as I triumphantly pulled out my crafting kit. "Ladies, I have two words for you: Glitter. Bomb."

I didn't even feel slightly guilty as I passed out tiny tubes of glitter to each girl. After being tortured for what felt like forever, I was giving myself a free pass to return the favor. Plus, the birthday girl can do what she wants, even if it's to the birthday boy, right?

We carefully tiptoed into Winston's bedroom, trying to be extra quiet. When we saw he was dead asleep, we went to work. We started sprinkling the glitter onto him and over his sheets, trying to get it done quickly and quietly so he wouldn't wake up.

Just before we escaped, Maren dumped some extra glitter into Winston's hair. "Sorry, Win," she whispered with a smile. Once back in the safety of my room, we all collapsed onto the bed in hysterical laughter.

"I'd say you got your revenge!" said Delaney, high-fiving me. "Best Share or Dare game *ever.*"

It had been an eventful evening, so we decided to pop in a chick flick and relax. By the time it was over, it was almost midnight, which would usually have been pretty early for us. However, tomorrow was a big day, so we decided to call it a night and hit the tents.

"Oh, um, about that," said Zoey. "We actually brought our own king-sized suede air bed."

Franny nodded, adding, "You didn't *really* think we'd sleep in a tent, did you?" Ahh, some things would never change.

Sophie piled on. "Is there room for a third in that king? I'm not really the outdoorsy type," she explained. Franny and Zoey agreed. The three of them seemed relieved.

At first, I felt a little bummed that the other girls weren't feelin' the whole tent thing, but then I realized it would be just us Sleepover Girls in the tent. And that made me one happy camper! The four of us headed out to the yard with flashlights in hand. Before we crawled into the tent, Ashley stopped us for a second. "I think we need to sing to Willow," she said with a big smile on her face.

The girls whispered the birthday song to me as lively as they could without waking up the neighbors, and it felt magical. When they were done, Maren saw me admiring the sky and pointed to the brightest star she could find. "Make a wish!" she urged me.

Zoey's wish from earlier floated into my mind. So instead of wishing something about Jacob, I wished that my friends and I would never stop having sleepovers, not even when we turned old and gray. (Maybe we'd get a little more sophisticated with it, calling it a "girls' getaway" or something.)

After a few ghost stories and flashlight shadow puppets in the tent, we fell asleep. I slept so peacefully that I almost forgot about our little "glitter bombing" incident. That is, until the girls and I were hanging out at the breakfast nook and Winston stumbled in, glitter trailing behind him and falling from his clothes and hair.

"Winston Keys, why is there glitter all over my clean kitchen?" asked my mom, looking pretty annoyed.

"Why don't you ask the glitter patrol over here? My bed looks like a disco ball," huffed Winston. "Lucky for you guys, I was going to get all gilded anyway for my C3PO costume. But still! Not okay."

My mom stood in front of us, clearly not happy. "Totally not okay," she said, staring me down. "There's a lot that needs to happen before the party starts, and cleaning up glitter is *not* on the approved to-do list. Willow, I think you'll be joining your brother on cleanup duty — and that includes washing his sheets."

I gulped. I was in trouble, but it was worth it to see Win in all his glittery glory. And she was right about one thing — it was party day!

After we gulped down our green smoothies, I bid all of the girls goodbye so they could go home and get ready. (No lounging around watching cartoons for us this morning.) As for me, well, I had about three hours of cleaning, decorating, and party prep to do. But first, it was time to draw a truce with the Win man.

I knocked on his door, trying to be heard over the handheld vacuum he was running over his bed. (Oops.)

"Winston!" I yelled, finally getting him to turn it off. "I just wanted to say I'm sorry for pranking you. Let me do that. It's the least I can do."

"Gladly," he said, handing it over to me. "Are we even now? I don't want to wake up tomorrow to makeup all over me."

I giggled. "Yes, totally even," I said. "Twinsies for life. Truce?"

He pulled my ponytail instead of taking my extended hand. "Truce."

All was right in twin world again . . . for now, anyway. Now it was time to get this party started!

chapter Ten

My stomach was doing backflips as the hand on the clock inched closer to 5:30. The "mixing and mingling" part of playing hostess didn't exactly come naturally to me, which was why I was so grateful that the Sleepover Girls had come early to help me greet everyone and get in the party mix.

"Willow, your house looks amazing!" exclaimed Ashley, surveying the room admiringly.

I had to admit she was right. We'd set up blacklights to give the space an eerie glow, and the decorations had all come together perfectly to create a "haunted house" feel. Maren's idea to have the witchy legs dangling from the chimney was incredible. A big sign reading "Eat, Drink, and Be Scary" hung over the treat table, which had everything from our pumpkin cupcakes to mummy-wrapped hot dogs to our cheese ghost. Plus, my mom had set out pumpkin swirls as the signature drink. The spooky music playlist Win and I'd made topped off the party atmosphere.

"Yep, just add guests and we're good to go," said my mom, taking a deep breath. She and my dad had really gone above and beyond to help us get ready. I definitely owed them one!

She didn't have to wait long — people started pouring in just after 5:30. Some of the girls from my homeroom showed up first, followed by a pack of Win's friends (including Jacob dressed as a pirate. Dreamy!). It was really fun to see all of the costumes, from Harry Potter to a fortune teller. Franny and Zoey were next, dressed as "Bread" and "Butter"!

I giggled at their creative costume. "Have fun but don't get 'spread' too thin," I joked as they made their way into the party. It felt good to be friendlier with them. Even if we weren't necessarily best friends, we'd never forget our shared campout experience.

I'd been a little worried that people would just sit around twiddling their thumbs, but that wasn't the case at all. People were already having fun with the apple bobbing station my dad had set up in the atrium. In fact, Tommy Miller even stuck his head all the way in and then shook water all over everyone, much to the Prickly Pair's dismay.

People were also going crazy over our photo booth, which was basically just a big empty picture frame and a Polaroid camera, along with props like my jack-o-lantern grins. Winston and Delaney posed together for a *Star Wars* shot, and they really looked the part! (Though I think he wished he was posing with the Pink Power Ranger instead.)

I was perched on my dad's recliner talking to Ashley when Jacob came up behind her and started spinning her Twister hat. She swatted at him, but he kept running past her. "OMG!" she exclaimed. "He won't stop doing that."

She slid into the recliner next to me and cupped her hand over my ear. "This is really weird, but I think Jacob might like me," she whispered. "He asked me if I might want to go to the movies sometime."

My heart sunk. *Of course* he'd been digging on Ashley this whole time. Had there ever been any question? I tried not to show that I was disappointed, but Ashley picked right up on it. "Oh, Willow, you don't like him, right?" she asked. Always preferring to keep things private, I hadn't really confided my crush in anyone other than Win. "I feel like such a jerk."

"Well, kinda sorta," I admitted, self-consciously clutching my Lady Liberty torch. "But you should go out with him! He's so cute — at least one of us can have him."

I could tell she felt really bad. "No way," she said. "We girls gotta stick together. And, if it makes you feel any better, I heard Grant's crushing on Zoey. So we can form an 'unrequited love' club or something."

"Deal," I told her, linking pinkies. I wasn't going to let this ruin my birthday. And suddenly, I got a huge case of the giggles as it hit me: Maren and Winston, the most unlikely couple of all, were the only ones that actually had mutual feelings for each other. "Who needs boys, anyway?"

We both looked over at Jacob and Tommy, who were busy chasing people around with silly string, and said at the same time, "Not us!"

The afternoon flew by as we went through all of our planned activities, like pumpkin carving and a candy scavenger hunt in the backyard. (Some of the Sleepover Girls got a ton of candy since they already knew the terrain after our flashlight tag game last night!) I got a little pang of sadness when I saw Jacob offer Ashley some of his Hershey's bars, but I'd already decided *nothing* was going to ruin my birthday — especially not a boy! I'd worked way too hard for anything to rain on my Halloween parade!

Plus, it was hard to dwell on that when there was so much other fun stuff to focus on. My favorite moment came when all the lights in the living room went out, and my mom and dad emerged from the kitchen with a tombstone-shaped cake topped with sparklers. For the second time in 24 hours, I got serenaded with the birthday song, except this time it was a *lot* louder.

"Happy birthday, Willow and Winston," everyone sang. "Happy birthday to you!"

And, as I looked at Win standing next to me, the Sleepover Girls whooping and cheering, the gift table piled high, and my cake-toting parents, it was hard to come up with a wish. Dream boy or not, my life was pretty dreamy just as it was.

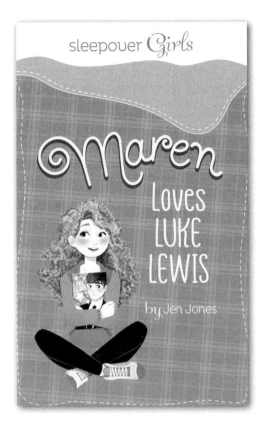

Can't get enough Sleepover Girls?
Check out the first chapter of

Maren Loves Luke Lewis

chapter One

My mom's giant Dr. Seuss hat came around the corner before she did. My mom sure knows how to make me smile.

"Happy half birthday, Mare-Bear!" she said, tilting the cake so the four of us could see her proud creation.

Since it was only half a cake, it was easy to see the bright rainbow layers in all of their glory — chocolate, red velvet, and vanilla. Pretty impressive for my mom, who is, as they say, a bit "domestically challenged" in the kitchen. On top of the cake, a star-shaped candle shone brightly atop cursive text that read simply, "Maren's a Star!"

Ashley stood up and started waving her hands as if conducting an imaginary orchestra. "Happy . . ."

"HALF!" Delaney and Willow shouted, giggling at the nerdiness of it all.

". . . birthday to you. Happy (HALF!) birthday to you. Happy (HALF!) birthday, dear Maren. Happy (HALF!) birthday to you!" As everyone finished the song and clapped, I had to smile. Although super cheesy, it was a memorable moment.

"Make a wish, Maren!" Willow urged, tucking a lock of long blond hair behind her ear. "Maybe it will come true."

"Well, that's easy," I replied, grinning. "I wish to become Mrs. Luke Lewis and have him serenade me every day and night for the rest of my life."

"You can't say your wish out loud or it won't come true," said Delaney.

"I don't care. It's worth saying Mrs. Luke Lewis out loud," I said dreamily.

Pursing my lips, I leaned forward and blew out the candle with a flourish. The girls laughed, and my mom rolled her eyes.

If you're wondering who Luke Lewis is, you obviously haven't listened to the radio or watched YouTube or looked at any popular magazines in, oh, forever.

Luke Lewis is the most amazing guitar-toting, hipster-haired pop singer of all time. And the coolest thing? Luke actually grew up in Valley View, our hometown! Yep, he even went to the same middle school we attend. I like to pretend my desk was his back in the day. Hey, a girl can dream.

"How about you finish sixth grade before you run off to marry a pop star?" said my mom good-naturedly. She grabbed the cake so she could go cut it in the kitchen.

"Ahh, that reminds me," said Ash, reaching into her oversized striped tote. "This may not be as good as a marriage license, but I have something for you."

She handed me a small rectangular package wrapped in polka-dot paper. After I eagerly tore it open, I couldn't help but laugh at what was inside. It was a framed magnetic photo of me and Luke Lewis! She'd taken a pic from our school dance and Photoshopped my body next to his in a red carpet photo.

"Ash, this is amazing!" I said, holding it up to my chest so Delaney and Willow could see. "This will make the perfect finishing touch for my locker. Or should we start calling it my Luke-r?"

Ashley giggled at my bad joke. "Roman helped me Photoshop it," she said. "I guess having a bunch of older brothers *does* come in handy sometimes."

Ash was one of five kids in a big Italian family; since her sister Josie was off at college, she was the only girl in her house. For such a girly girl, it was often boy overload for Ashley. But, like she said, there were plenty of perks, too, including meeting older boys.

"My turn," said Willow, handing me a gift bag with a swirly "M" on the outside. I had no doubt she'd stenciled it herself. The girl was so crafty. It always impressed me.

I opened the bag to unveil a chevron-patterned, hand-knit iPad cozy. But before I could admire it, Ashley snatched it from my hand.

"Are you kidding me?" she exclaimed. "Wills, this is above and beyond. You have to make me one for my birthday. Or half birthday. Or just for any day."

It really was above and beyond, but I'd learned not to expect anything less from Willow. She blushed as I gave her a hug. "Thanks, chiquita," I told her. "You rock! My iPad is going to be better dressed than me!"

It was Delaney's turn. She seemed a bit embarrassed. "Well, this pales in comparison, but here you go!"

She pulled a box from her own bag and handed it to me. "Sorry I didn't have time to wrap it. I was at the animal shelter all day." Delaney was a regular volunteer at Valley View Animal Rescue, which is where she had actually found her adorable dog, Frisco. Frisco could turn any person into a dog lover!

A closer look at the box revealed that it was actually a board game. I loved board games, so this was perfect!

"Oooh, Say Anything," I said, reading the label. "I should be good at that." It was no secret that I wasn't afraid to speak my mind!

"Yeah, we should definitely play later," said Ashley. "But not before cake!" I followed her gaze to the patio door, where my mom was coming out with slices of rainbow cake for all of us.

"You guys, thank you so much. You totally didn't have to get me gifts — it's not even my real birthday. Having you sleep over is more than enough."

And it was. Our weekly sleepovers had become the thing that got me through the school day on Friday — scratch that, the thing I looked forward to most every week!

On the rare occasion that we couldn't have our Friday sleepover, I was known to be a little crabby. (You can ask my mom.) Our sleepovers had earned us the nickname "The Sleepover

Girls" at school. It was definitely a fitting name for our fierce foursome.

The funny thing was that our sleepovers had started all because of me, in a way. My mom is the editor-in-chief of a travel mag called *Fly Girls*, and she's jet-setting much of the time for her job. (Sometimes I get to go with her! I'll never forget our South African safari.) Since she is gone a lot, Delaney's mom started watching me on weekends sometimes, and the two of us always had a blast. When my mom later returned the favor, Willow and Ashley joined in the fun. From there, the Sleepover Girls were born!

Even funnier was the fact that the half-birthday tradition had started because of my mom's job, too. Every year, her magazine hosts a big travel writing conference in New York City. It just happens to fall on the same weekend as my birthday. (I know, bummer, right?) Luckily, it's become an excuse to go visit my dad down in San Diego. A California birthday? Yes, please, says this Oregon girl.

So now I get to spend half birthdays with my mom, and my actual birthday with my dad and stepfamily. Of course, I'd rather that my parents were still together, but what are ya gonna do? At least my stepfamily is cool, and both my parents seem a lot happier now than they did when they were married.

As if on cue, my mom bent down and kissed the top of my head. "Love you, Red," she said, tousling my curly fire-red hair and pulling a hot pink envelope from her pocket. "You know I couldn't resist just one more half-birthday surprise."

Say what? We'd already done a manicure day earlier this week, plus the cake and sleepover. As usual, my mom had gone overboard. But I'm never one to turn down a gift! I ripped open the envelope and almost lost my breath when I saw what was inside.

"No you *didn't!*" I gasped, as my mood went from an already-high ten to off the charts. In front of me was a set of shiny Luke Lewis concert tickets to his *totally sold-out* show. The one I'd spent a whole afternoon on Ticketmaster trying to get. The one I'd called in trying to win radio giveaways a million times with no luck. I held the tickets up in the air, fanning them out so the girls could see, too. We all started jumping up and down and screaming.

"Ms. Taylor, you are my favorite person in life!" yelled Ashley, giving her a squeeze. My mom grinned. "I couldn't let Luke Lewis come back to Valley View and not help you girls get in on the fun," she said.

Blown away, I lifted my fizzy passion fruit drink to signify a toast. "This calls for a serious shout-out," I said, beaming at my mom. "To my awesome mom, and to another great *half* birthday that's been a *whole* lotta fun." Maybe Luke Lewis wasn't my husband (yet), but getting to see him sing in person was second best. And as we all clinked glasses, I knew deep down that having the best BFFs ever made my life more than complete!

What is your ideal party theme?
Take this quiz to find out and start planning!

1. What is your favorite hobby?
   a) spending time with animals
   b) hiking
   c) crafting
   d) shopping

2. What is your favorite food?
   a) pizza
   b) s'mores and hot dogs
   c) fruit and salads
   d) appetizers — any and all

3. Which state would you most like to visit?
   a) Montana
   b) Colorado
   c) California
   d) New York

4. What does your ideal day involve?
   a) riding horses
   b) playing outside
   c) swimming
   d) sleeping

5. What is your favorite season?
   a) spring
   b) fall
   c) summer
   d) winter

6. Pick your favorite style.
   a) casual
   b) sporty
   c) earthy
   d) trendy

7. You flip on the TV. What do you watch?
   a) anything with animals
   b) sports
   c) No TV for me!
   d) a chick flick

8. What is the best part of a party?
   a) the food
   b) the games
   c) the music
   d) the gossip

9. What is your favorite subject in school?
   a) science
   b) gym
   c) art
   d) media

Got mostly "a" answers? Like Delaney, a pet party is perfect for you.

Got mostly "b" answers? You and Maren both love a camping/outdoorsy party.

Got mostly "c" answers? A relaxing pool party is for you, just like Willow.

Got mostly "d" answers? You and Ashley love to be pampered at a spa party.

Want to throw a sleepover party your friends will never forget?

Let the Sleepover Girls help!
The Sleepover Girls Craft titles
are filled with easy recipes, crafts,
and other how-tos combined with
step-by-step instructions and colorful
photos that will help you throw the
best sleepover party ever! Grab all
four of the Sleepover Girls Craft titles
before your next party so you can create
unforgettable memories.

About the Author
Jen Jones

Using her past experience as a writer for E! Online, Jen Jones has written more than forty books about celebrities, crafting, cheerleading, fashion, and just about any other obsession a girl in middle school could have — including her popular *Team Cheer!* series for Capstone. Jen lives in Los Angeles.